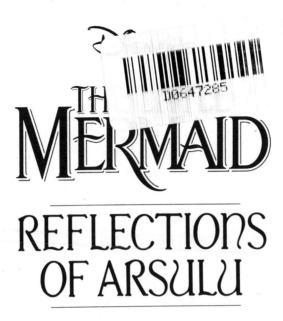

THE
MERMAID

REFLECTIONS
OF ARSULU

by Marilyn Kaye

illustrations by Fred Marvin

DISNEP
PRESS

NEW YORK

Books in The Little Mermaid series:

For Anna Burstein

Produced by arrangement with Chardiet Unlimited, Inc.

Library of Congress Catalog Card Number: 92-53935

ISBN: 1-56282-248-9

FIRST EDITION

3 5 7 9 10 8 6 4 2

In the deepest, darkest part of the ocean, Ursula the Sea Witch prowled around her gloomy cave. She was in a very bad mood.

Her pet eels, Flotsam and Jetsam, were curled up in a corner, listening to her complaints.

"Once, it was *I* who ruled the kingdom of the sea," she grumbled. "Once, it was *I* who had power over all sea creatures. Then that wretched Triton took it all away from me!" As she uttered the name of the Sea King, the eels raised their heads and hissed.

"Flotsam! Jetsam!" she declared. "The time has come for me to reclaim my kingdom and put an end to Triton." She clenched her fists and gritted her teeth. "But how? How? Triton watches everything. He sees all that happens in the kingdom. If I make even the slightest move, he'll know about it immediately. How can I possibly recapture my throne?"

She paced the cave furiously. "There simply must be a way to distract him and snatch control before he knows what's happening. But how can I do that?"

Ursula considered the possibilities. "Perhaps I could send him an invitation to visit a remote sea?" She shook her head. "No, that wouldn't work. Triton is much too smart to fall for that."

"Maybe I can create a tidal wave in a distant part of his kingdom. Then, when he leaves the palace to come to the aid of his subjects, I can sneak in." She shook her head again. "No, no, no. He would suspect me, and he would most certainly be on guard."

She gnashed her teeth and glared at her

pets. "Why do you not help me, you good-for-nothing eels?" she screeched.

Flotsam slithered across the cave and wrapped himself around Ursula's crystal ball.

Ursula snarled at him. "Yes, Flotsam. I can spy on Triton through my crystal ball anytime I want. But what good will it do? It won't help me take over the kingdom."

Jetsam joined Flotsam at the ball. Together they crawled around it.

"Well, all right. I suppose it's better than doing nothing," Ursula said. She dragged her enormous body over to the crystal ball. Muttering a few magic words, she stroked the ball, then peered deeply into it.

The images were blurry at first, but when they cleared, Ursula could see King Triton and his seven daughters gathered around the dinner table in the royal dining hall. The mermaids were laughing merrily, and King Triton was beaming at them.

The sight of the happy royal family did nothing to improve Ursula's foul mood.

"What did you do today, my dears?" King Triton asked his seven beautiful daughters as they were enjoying their dinner.

Alana spoke up. "I found a crab with a broken claw and fixed it for him," she said.

Her sisters looked at her in admiration. "That was nice of you," Ariel said. "You're so good with all the creatures."

Triton nodded in approval. "As princesses, it is especially important for you to show kindness to every creature and merperson in all the kingdom."

"I had my ballet class," Aquata announced.

"And I watched her," Andrina piped up. "Aquata was the best one there!"

"I believe that someone has a birthday coming up," Triton remarked with a smile. Adella giggled.

"We haven't forgotten," Arista said. She winked at Ariel, and Ariel smiled. Her sisters knew that Ariel had been working all month on a beautiful coral sculpture for Adella's birthday present. It was going to be a big surprise.

Alana turned to Arista and spoke in a whisper. "I don't know what to get for Adella. Do you?"

"I can't think of anything she doesn't already have," Arista whispered back. "Maybe we can go shopping and get something for her together."

"That was an excellent dinner," King Triton stated, patting his stomach. "Cook has certainly outdone himself."

The mermaids giggled. "It's Cook's day off," Adella said. "We made the dinner!"

"We didn't want to tell you until we found out if you liked it!" Andrina laughed.

King Triton was amazed. "*My* daughters made this delicious seaweed stew?"

They nodded. "We all worked together," Arista told him. "I had the recipe from a cooking course I took last year."

King Triton gazed at them fondly. "Ah, my daughters, I am so proud of you. Not simply because you made this stew. It pleases me that you all get along so well together. I know that I am not always able to give you the attention you deserve."

"You give us plenty of attention, Father," Ariel assured him, and swam over to give him a hug.

King Triton patted her head. "Not as much as I would like to, though. Governing the kingdom takes up so much of my time. At least it is a comfort to know that I don't have to worry about how my family is getting along. I know that you love and help each other."

"Of course we do," Alana said. "We're a family!"

"But there are some families that don't get

along as well as you do," the King said.

"I feel sorry for them," Attina said.

King Triton agreed. "Family is very important. Never forget that! Why, being a father is more important to me than being king!"

Back in the dark, gloomy cave, the images in the crystal ball began to fade. Ursula could conjure them up again, but she had no need to see or hear more. She rubbed her plump hands together, and her lips curled into a very nasty grin.

"So family is more important to him than his kingdom," she said. "That gives me an idea! Now I know what will distract him!" She clapped her hands in evil glee. "Those miserable mermaids are dear to his heart, eh? Then that's where I shall strike—at his heart!"

She turned to her eels in triumph. "Flotsam! Jetsam! I have my plan." Her mean eyes glittered. "He wishes he had more time to act like a father? Well, I can grant that wish. He'll have plenty of time to play daddy—when he's no longer king!"

3

Adella was taking a leisurely swim through the waters. Actually, she was hoping she might encounter a certain merman she'd had her eye on for weeks. His name was Tristan, and she thought he was adorable.

As she swam, Adella noticed a school of goldfish coming toward her. "Good morning, Princess," they called.

"Good morning," Adella replied. She took a moment to examine her reflection in their shiny scales. Yes, she could see that she looked pretty. She wished her long, flowing black hair was shinier, but that was her only problem.

She swam along slowly, but she didn't see Tristan anywhere.

Someone else caught her eye, though. Resting on a rock nearby was a mermaid Adella had never seen before. How strange—she thought she knew all the mermaids who lived in this part of the sea.

The stranger had long blond hair that was so shiny it sparkled. Her skin was clear and smooth and her lips full and red, and her eyes were the prettiest Adella had ever seen. Even from a distance, Adella was amazed at how vibrant they were. They were as blue as the sea.

Of course, Adella would have preferred to see a certain handsome merman rather than this mermaid, but she was interested all the same. She drew closer to get a better look at the stranger.

"Good morning," Adella said.

"Hello," said the mermaid. She smiled in a friendly way, but Adella was a bit surprised. Merpeople usually addressed her as Princess. Maybe this mermaid didn't know who *she* was, either.

"I am Princess Adella," she said, awaiting a response. She was pleased when the mermaid rose from her rock and bowed.

"Oh my! The daughter of the great King Triton! How do you do, Princess Adella. My name is Arsulu. I am a traveler passing through your kingdom. I stopped here to rest."

"Where are you going?" Adella asked.

"I am roaming the seas," Arsulu told her, "looking for someone."

"Who?"

"A young merman," Arsulu replied. Her blue eyes were sad. "We were engaged to be married," she explained. "But he angered Ursula the Sea Witch, and she chased him from our waters. I haven't seen him since, and I don't know where he could be." She hung her head as a tear trickled down her cheek.

What a sad, romantic story, Adella thought. "Do you think he may be somewhere in our waters?" she asked.

Arsulu sighed. "I hope so," she said. "I have been searching for him for many months and am so tired from all the traveling."

Adella admired the graceful way Arsulu moved when she spoke. Her voice was like music—so soft and sweet. Everything about her was elegant and poised. Adella looked around nervously. This was definitely someone she did *not* want Tristan to meet!

Suddenly two lovely fish appeared from behind Arsulu. "Aren't those angelfish?" Adella asked.

Arsulu glanced down at the fish and smiled. "Yes. They are my pets. They go with me everywhere."

"They're beautiful," Adella said, admiring their cherubic faces.

"And in my long journey, they are my only friends," Arsulu said sadly.

That's strange, Adella thought to herself. Surely a beautiful mermaid like Arsulu would have *lots* of friends. Why, *I* have dozens of best friends, she thought, and *I'm* even prettier than *she* is!

Anyway, Arsulu *did* seem so sad and lonely. With six sisters always around, Adella was never lonely. Suddenly she had an idea—why not introduce Arsulu to her sisters? It would be a nice gesture, Adella thought. And they would certainly be impressed with her new and gorgeous friend!

"Arsulu, would you like to meet my sisters?" she asked.

"Oh, yes!" Arsulu said, brightening a bit. She gathered up a large silk bag that was lying by her side and motioned to her fish that it was time to move on.

Side by side the two mermaids moved through the water toward the palace. The angelfish followed closely behind.

"How many sisters do you have?" Arsulu asked as they swam.

"Six."

"And are they all as pretty as you?"

Adella flushed with pleasure. "Well, we're all quite different from each other, but we're very close. Do you have any sisters or brothers?" Adella asked, hopeful that it was *handsome* brothers Arsulu had.

"No," Arsulu replied sadly. "I always wished for a sister or brother when I was younger, but my parents died a long time ago. My aunt and uncle raised me."

The poor mermaid! Adella thought. No wonder she's so lonely. First she loses her parents, then her merman. She definitely needs some cheering up. "Oh, look!" Adella said, pointing. "Here comes my oldest sister now."

She introduced Aquata to Arsulu, and Arsulu

bowed again. "I am honored to meet you, Princess Aquata. In my travels I frequently hear of the beauty and grace of King Triton's eldest daughter."

Aquata was clearly pleased. "Why, thank you," she said. "You are very kind. I wish I could stay and speak with you more, but I'm afraid I must be going. This is my day to visit the oyster orphanage."

"How generous of you to take time away from your busy schedule to help unfortunate orphans!" Arsulu declared.

Aquata nodded modestly. "I hope to see you again soon, Arsulu."

Adella and Arsulu continued on. They were about to enter the gates of the palace when Andrina burst out, riding on the back of a sea horse.

"Giddyap!" she screeched. "Whoopee!"

"Andrina! Wait! Stop for a minute!" Adella hoped her sister's wild riding hadn't frightened Arsulu.

"Whoa!" Andrina yelled. "Hi, Adella. Who's your friend?"

"This is Arsulu. She's traveling through our sea."

"Hi," Andrina said cheerfully.

"Hello," Arsulu replied. "What a lovely horse! And you ride him so well!"

Andrina was pleased by the compliment. "Thank you!" she said. "Would you like to ride him?"

Before Arsulu could answer, Adella took her by the arm. "Maybe later," she told Andrina. "Right now I'm going to give Arsulu a tour of the palace."

"It was nice to meet you, Arsulu!" Andrina called as she rode away.

Inside the palace Adella found Alana and Arista in Arista's bedroom. When Adella entered the room, her sisters were huddled close, whispering. Adella cleared her throat, and they quickly stopped talking. "I'd like you to meet my new friend, Arsulu," she said, smiling proudly that she knew such a beautiful, well-mannered mermaid.

Alana couldn't take her eyes off Arsulu's angelfish. "Are those yours?" she asked. "They're gorgeous! I never heard of anyone having angelfish for pets." She reached out to pet one of them, but the fish drew back.

"I thought angelfish were supposed to

be friendly," Alana said, frowning.

"They're not used to strangers," Arsulu apologized. She shook a finger at the fish. "Naughty, naughty! Be nice!"

Immediately the fish moved toward Alana and rubbed against her scales in a friendly way.

"Amazing," Alana murmured. "You're awfully good with sea creatures." She gazed at Arsulu in admiration.

"So what were you two whispering about?" Adella asked suspiciously.

Alana and Arista exchanged looks. "Well, if you must know, we're trying to decide what to get you for your birthday."

"Ooh! Tell me what you've decided," Adella said eagerly.

"No," said Alana. "It has to be a surprise. Besides, we don't know yet. We may chip in and get one present together, or we may get two."

"Perhaps I can help you," Arsulu said. "I love shopping, and I must say I have rather good taste."

Arista and Alana looked at each other in delight. "That would be great," Arista said. "We need all the help we can get!"

As Adella led Arsulu out of the room, she

could hear Alana saying, "Isn't she sweet!" Adella beamed. She was proud to show off her new friend.

Adella took Arsulu to meet Attina, who was, as usual, reading. After Adella made the introductions, Arsulu motioned to her that they should leave. "I can see that Attina is very busy," she said. "I don't want to disturb her."

"Oh, that's all right," Attina said, putting down her book. "I've just finished." She frowned and pointed to her bookshelf. "I've read all those already," she said. "Now I have nothing left to read."

"I have a book you might like," Arsulu said. Reaching into her silk bag, she pulled out a book and handed it to Attina.

"Oh, yes!" Attina cried in glee. "*Huckleberry's Fin!* I've been wanting to read this!"

"You may keep it if you like," Arsulu said.

"Thank you!" Within seconds, Attina was happily engrossed in the book.

From down the hallway came the sound of singing. Arsulu's eyes widened. "Who is that?" she asked.

"That's our youngest sister, Ariel," Adella

said. She took Arsulu to meet her.

"What a beautiful voice you have!" Arsulu gushed at Ariel.

"Thank you," Ariel said shyly. "Are those angelfish?"

"Yes. They're Arsulu's pets," Adella said.

"How nice," Ariel said, reaching out to pet one. This time Arsulu's angelfish seemed happy to be petted.

"Tell me, Ariel," Arsulu said. "Where did you learn to sing so beautifully?"

Embarrassed, Ariel just shrugged. "I don't know."

"I could listen to you sing all day!" Arsulu said. "I love to sing, too. Do you know 'Whispering Water'?" She sang a few lines from the song. Adella was impressed. Arsulu's singing was as sweet as Ariel's.

When Arsulu finished, she turned to Adella. "You are so lucky to have such wonderful sisters. I envy you. How glorious it must be to live here, with such a lovely family." The longing in her voice was clear, and it touched Adella's heart.

"Arsulu," she said, "why don't you stay here with us? At least until you have found your merman," she added.

"Here?" Arsulu's large eyes became huge. "In the palace?"

"Yes," Adella said. "Stay for as long as you like. We'd love to have you."

Arsulu smiled. "Adella, this is really so kind of you. Thank you, I would love to stay here with you and your generous family."

Adella clapped her hands together. "Great! Come, I'll show you to the guest room."

She started down the hall with Arsulu, but Ariel called her back. "May I speak with you for a second, Adella?" she asked. "In private?" Ariel looked concerned.

"Are you sure you want to invite her to stay here?" Ariel asked. "She's a total stranger, Adella. You don't know anything about her. And with Father away tonight, do you think you should ask her to stay without his permission?"

"Oh, don't be such a worrier, Ariel," Adella said. "Arsulu's *so* nice. Anyone can see that. Alana, Andrina, Attina—everyone likes her. Besides, remember what Father said yesterday. As members of the royal family, we have to be particularly kind to everyone in the kingdom. Well, that's what I'm doing. Being *kind*. I'm sure Father won't mind." Then Adella smirked.

"Ariel, are you jealous?" she asked.

"Jealous?" Ariel asked. "No. Why would I be jealous?"

"Because Arsulu's so pretty, she sings so well, and everyone likes her."

"That's silly," Ariel protested. "I hardly know her! I'm not jealous!"

"Then be nice to her," Adella warned. "She's lonely, and she needs friends." Adella explained Arsulu's sad story to Ariel, and Ariel immediately felt guilty.

"I'm sorry, Adella," Ariel said. "Of course Arsulu should stay with us."

Adella swam back and joined her friend, and the two mermaids made their way to the royal bedchambers.

What a depressing story, Ariel thought. Although she'd complained many times in the past about having *too many* sisters, Ariel suddenly felt very happy to be part of such a big, loving family. And with a swish of her tail, she took off for the cave to do some more work on Adella's birthday present.

At breakfast the next morning, the mermaids told King Triton about Arsulu.

"Oh, Father, you must meet her," Adella exclaimed. "She's so beautiful!"

"And elegant and charming!" Arista added.

"And she's very kind," Attina said.

"Even to sea creatures," Alana chimed in.

They went on and on, raving about their guest, but Ariel could tell that their father wasn't listening very carefully. "That is very nice, my daughters," he said halfheartedly. "But I'm afraid I won't get the chance to meet your new friend. I must leave right now and tend to a dispute elsewhere in the kingdom." With a sigh, he left the palace.

"I so wanted Father to meet Arsulu," Adella whined when Triton was gone. "Where is she, anyway?"

In answer to her question, Arsulu appeared in the dining room. "Good morning! And what a lovely morning it is," she said. "I'm sorry to be late for breakfast, but I was so comfortable in your guest room and so tired from my journey that I overslept." She gazed around the room. "Where is your father?"

"He had to leave suddenly," Aquata said. "There was a problem he needed to attend to."

"Father knows everything that goes on in the kingdom," Arista boasted. "Nothing escapes his eye!"

"Yes," Arsulu said. "He has a reputation for being a great leader."

Aquata rose from the table. "If you'll excuse me, I have some errands to run," she said. Then she turned to her sisters. "Be sure to check the chart to see what responsibilities you have for today," she said. She summoned a servant to call for her carriage and went to wait for its arrival.

When she was gone, Adella turned to Arsulu. "Arsulu, please tell me something," she said. "How do you make your hair so shiny?"

Arsulu smiled. "I have a special secret formula that I use every day. Would you like to try it?"

Adella nodded eagerly and sprang up from her chair. Ariel and Andrina joined her as she followed Arsulu to the guest room.

Arsulu pointed to a collection of bottles, jars, mixing bowls, and measuring cups that lined her dresser. "This is it," she said. "I would help you, but I must leave now in order to get an early start on my search." Her eyes misted over. "Perhaps today I shall find my beloved merman."

"How do you use this stuff?" Adella asked.

Arsulu pointed to the side of one of the jars. "Here are the directions," she said. "But you may need some help."

"I'll help her," Andrina offered.

"What a kind sister," Arsulu said. "Andrina, just be sure to follow the instructions very carefully."

"I want to try this right now," Adella said, grabbing the jar off the dresser. "You see, Arsulu, I too have an interest in a merman. I know that he goes to the royal garden every day to eat his lunch. Well, today I plan to meet him there!" She giggled. "Accidentally, of course."

Arsulu laughed. "How charming! And what is this special merman's name?"

"Tristan," Adella said breathlessly. Even the sound of his name made her blush.

Arsulu patted Adella's shoulder. "With my special formula you will look beautiful for Tristan." Then she turned to Andrina. "Remember," she warned. "Follow the instructions *exactly*." Blowing a kiss at the mermaids, she left.

Ariel settled down to watch as Andrina began to read the directions. "Let's see," Andrina said. "It says to mix four drops from this bottle with one cup of the stuff in this bottle." She did that. "Now, stir exactly six times." Ariel counted out loud as Andrina stirred.

"Maybe you should stir it one extra time," Adella suggested.

"No," Andrina said. "Arsulu said to follow the directions exactly. Now I'm supposed to add a teaspoon of this oil and two tablespoons of this cream."

"Isn't this awfully complicated for a hair potion?" Ariel asked.

"It's a special formula," Adella said. "Have you ever seen hair as shiny as Arsulu's?"

"It's definitely shiny," Ariel said. "In fact, it's so shiny, it doesn't look real."

"Of course it's real," Adella sniffed. "You're just jealous because your hair isn't as nice."

"I think this is ready," Andrina finally announced, peering into the bowl. "The directions say it should look like pudding. Ariel, does this look like pudding to you?"

Ariel looked. "Not like any pudding *I'd* want to eat."

"Hurry up!" Adella ordered. "I have to be ready by lunchtime."

Andrina began dripping the globby brown mixture over Adella's hair, covering it completely. "You have to leave it on for one hour," Andrina said, wrinkling her nose.

Ariel didn't particularly want to sit around and watch Adella's hair become shiny, so she went to her own bedroom, flopped down on her bed, and read a magazine.

An hour later, the peace and quiet of the palace was broken by a shrill scream. Ariel leapt up and raced down the hall. The shrieking grew louder as she approached the guest room.

Andrina was there, her jaw open wide in a state of shock. Adella was sobbing. Or *was* it Adella? Ariel almost didn't recognize her sister—her hair had turned completely green.

"What happened?" Ariel asked, staring at Adella in wide-eyed horror.

"My hair!" Adella shrieked. "My hair! Just look at my hair!"

"It's—it's green," Ariel stammered.

"I know it's green!" Adella yelled.

"How did it happen?" Ariel asked.

Adella pointed at Andrina. "It's all her fault! She didn't follow the directions properly!"

"Yes I did," Andrina replied.

"No you didn't!" Adella shot back. "You couldn't have followed the directions properly. It's supposed to be shiny—not green! Oh, what am I going to do?"

"You could wear a scarf," Andrina suggested.

That idea didn't go over very well with Adella. "Andrina, I'm furious with you! You did this on purpose!"

"That's crazy," Ariel said. "Why would Andrina do that on purpose?"

"Because—because she's always been jealous of my hair," Adella stated.

"Says who?" Andrina retorted.

"Don't fight," Ariel pleaded. "I'll see if I can find Arsulu. Maybe she knows how to fix your hair."

Ariel had to swim for quite a while before she spotted Arsulu resting on some sea grass, speaking to her angelfish. As Ariel got closer, she thought she heard Arsulu say, "Give this to Tristan." Tristan? Where had she heard that name before? Ariel wondered. She watched as the fish took off. Never mind, she told herself, she had more important things on her mind. She had to tell Arsulu about what had happened to Adella's hair.

"Arsulu!" Ariel called. "Come quick! Adella needs you."

Arsulu hurried back to the palace, where Adella and Andrina were still fighting with each other. "I hate you!" Adella was shouting when Ariel and Arsulu arrived.

"The feeling is mutual!" Andrina yelled as she swam off. With a loud bang, she slammed her bedroom door behind her.

"Oh dear," Arsulu said, examining Adella's hair. "Andrina must not have read the directions properly."

"What am I going to do?" Adella wailed.

"Don't worry," Arsulu said soothingly. "I'll fix it." Almost magically, with a few drops of this and that, Arsulu changed the color back to Adella's natural black.

"Oh, Arsulu, how can I thank you?" Adella cried. "You are now my dearest friend in the sea!"

"Now, go find your merman," Arsulu said, smiling. "I'm off to continue my search."

Adella took one more look in the mirror. "Oh, I'm so nervous," she exclaimed. "Wish me luck, Ariel!"

"Good luck, Adella," Ariel said as she

watched her sister leave the palace.

Carefully, so as not to mess her hair, Adella swam over to the royal garden to look for Tristan. She spotted him from afar having lunch in the gazebo.

But as she got closer, Adella realized that Tristan was not alone. She ducked behind a statue to spy on him. Who is that with him? she wondered. Then she gasped. "It's Aquata!" she said out loud.

Aquata was talking and laughing with the handsome merman. I can't believe Aquata is *flirting* with him! Adella thought angrily. She strained to hear the conversation.

"Yes, I'd love to go with you to the Fighting Fish concert," Aquata was saying. "They're my favorite band."

Adella felt sick. I was hoping he'd ask *me* to that concert! she thought to herself. I can't believe it, my own sister, stealing the merman I like!

Suddenly Adella noticed that Aquata was leaving the gazebo and swimming toward her. Adella clenched her fists when she saw the huge smile on her older sister's face. When Aquata was only a few feet away, Adella came out from behind the statue and confronted her. "What were you doing with him?" she demanded.

Aquata seemed surprised to see Adella there, but she was still so giddy from her meeting with Tristan that she didn't even ask why Adella was there. "It's all so strange, really," she explained. "I received a note from him this morning, asking me to meet him here."

"He sent you a note?" Adella asked in disbelief.

Aquata laughed. "He denies sending it, but who else would have done it? And the weird part is, he claims to have received a note from me! Isn't that strange?"

Adella stared at her in a fury. "Aquata!" she cried. "I never want to speak to you again!"

"What? Why?" Aquata asked in bewilderment. "What are you talking about?"

But Adella didn't answer. For the second time in an hour, she burst into tears. Whirling around, she swam angrily away.

Ariel didn't want to eat lunch at the palace. She didn't want to have to listen to any more bickering—it was giving her a big headache.

Instead, she swam over to the cave where she'd been making Adella's birthday present. On her way there, she passed Adella swimming fast and furiously with tears in her eyes.

"Oh, Ariel," she wailed. "Listen to what just happened!" Adella told her sister the whole story. "I'm so mad at Aquata!" she added. "I never want to speak to her again." She swam away.

Ariel felt bad for Adella. She knew how upset she must be. But the whole incident sounded so strange to begin with. It wasn't like Aquata to do something like that, Ariel thought.

At the cave, Ariel worked on the sculpture, carving the pink-and-white coral. It was really coming along beautifully. Adella will love this, she thought. Ariel just hoped all the quarreling would be over in time for Adella's birthday.

She stayed alone in the cave for a while, enjoying some quiet time by herself. When she finally returned to the palace, she saw Arista leaving with Arsulu.

"Oh, there you are, Ariel," Arista said. "Maybe *you* can tell us what's going on between Adella and Aquata."

"They both seem so upset," added Arsulu. "And angry."

Ariel told them about the garden and the merman.

"How awful!" Arista exclaimed. "That was mean of Aquata to go after the merman Adella likes."

"I don't think Aquata knew Adella liked him," Ariel said. "But somehow Aquata has the idea that *he* likes *her*."

"How strange," Arsulu said.

"Yes, it's very strange," Ariel repeated. "Where are you two going?"

"Shopping," Arista said, "for a birthday present for Adella. Arsulu is going to give me her opinion."

When Ariel went into the palace, she found Alana just outside the dining room, studying the Daily Royal Missions chart on the wall. The chart listed all the princesses' names and the kingdom responsibilities they had for that day.

"This is peculiar," Alana murmured. "I thought this was my day to visit the sea hospital. But look, the chart says it's Aquata's turn."

Ariel glanced at the chart. "You're right. But what's so peculiar about that?"

"Well, I checked the chart just after breakfast this morning," Alana said. "And I thought I saw *my* name there. I was about to leave for the hospital about half an hour ago, when I happened to look at the chart again." She shrugged. "I guess I was wrong. Anyway, now I have my afternoon free. Ariel, come up to my room. I want to show you something."

They swam up to Alana's bedroom. "Look," she said. "This is the present I'm giving Adella for her birthday."

She held up a beautiful jewelry box inlaid with pink seashells and pearls. "Oh, it's perfect!" Ariel said. She took it from Alana and opened it. "Wow!" she exclaimed. "There's a mirror under the lid. It's very pretty."

"I was lucky to find it," Alana said. "Arsulu went shopping with me this morning."

Just then they heard their father's booming voice.

"Alana! Where are you?"

Alana looked at Ariel worriedly. "Father's back, and he sounds angry. I wonder why."

"I don't know," Ariel said. "Let's find out."

They swam down to the dining room, where King Triton was waiting impatiently.

"Alana," he said, "why aren't you over at the hospital? I've just received word that you hadn't shown up. I'm very disappointed in you. The children's ward was expecting you."

"But Father," Alana protested. "It's Aquata's turn to go today."

Aquata appeared just in time to hear her name. "My turn to do what?" she asked.

"Visit the hospital," Alana said.

"No it isn't. It's your turn," she said sharply to Alana.

King Triton grew more impatient. "Bickering isn't going to help the sick children," he said. "I suggest you decide just whose turn it is to go, and go!" With that, he turned and left.

"Aquata, I saw *your* name on the chart just a little while ago," Alana insisted.

"Oh, really?" Aquata went to the chart. "Well, it's not there now."

Alana and Ariel joined her. Sure enough, the chart clearly stated that it was Alana's day to visit the sea hospital.

"That's weird," Alana said. "Ariel, you saw Aquata's name on the chart, didn't you?"

Ariel scratched her head. "I *thought* I did."

"You're just trying to get out of going to the hospital," Aquata snapped.

"I am not," Alana shot back. "*You* are."

Their voices rose. "Don't be so childish, Alana!" Aquata shouted.

"Don't be so obnoxious!" Alana yelled back. "I *did* see your name!"

"That's a lie!" Aquata screeched.

Ariel gasped. She'd never heard her sisters talk like this to each other. It was very upsetting, not to mention noisy. She tried to get them to stop, but they ignored her. Frustrated, she fled to her bedroom, where she was guaranteed some quiet. Only she didn't have it for long.

This time the yelling came from Alana's room. What now? Ariel wondered. She went down the hall to see.

"I can't believe it!" Arista exclaimed. She was staring at the jewelry box Alana had bought for Adella. "You can't give her that!"

It was then that Ariel noticed the identical jewelry box in Arista's hands. "You bought the same gift?" she asked.

"Yes. And Alana will have to find something else to give Adella," Arista said.

"I will not!" Alana stated. "I bought my jewelry box first!" They started shrieking at each other again.

"Stop it!" Ariel cried out. "Both of you!" She couldn't bear this any longer. She swam out of the room, covering her ears.

Ariel decided that maybe she ought to talk

to Aquata. Surely, as the oldest, Aquata could see that all this fighting wasn't natural.

But as she neared Aquata's room, Ariel heard Arsulu's voice coming from inside. She hid behind the door and strained to hear the conversation.

"It must be so difficult," Arsulu was saying. "Being the oldest is such a responsibility."

"No kidding," Aquata replied. "Honestly, sometimes my sisters can be so . . ."

"Immature?" Arsulu suggested.

"Exactly," Aquata said.

"You're expected to be in charge," Arsulu continued. "But they don't listen to you. It's not fair."

"You know, you're right," Aquata said. "I never thought about it that way before. It *isn't* fair. You're so understanding, Arsulu."

Just then Arista and Alana swam past Ariel and burst into Aquata's room. Ariel followed them in.

"What do *you* want?" Aquata asked harshly.

"I bought this jewelry box for Adella," Arista said, "and Alana bought the same one. Even the inside is the same." They both opened their boxes to reveal the mirrors inside.

Suddenly Arsulu became flustered. She rose and swam to the door. "Uh, excuse me, but I just remembered something I must do," she said. She rushed out of the room, but nobody even noticed. They were too busy bickering.

"I bought the present first," Alana told Aquata. "But Arista says—"

She didn't get any further. Aquata glared at her. "I'm not interested in your silly little problems," she snapped. "And I'm tired of being responsible for you . . . you . . . *children*. Get out of my room!"

Arista burst into tears and flew out the door.

"Fine!" Alana yelled, swimming out right behind her.

Aquata looked at Ariel. "You, too, Ariel!" she yelled.

Dazed, Ariel swam out of Aquata's room. From down the hall she could hear Arista, still crying. She couldn't blame her. She felt like crying herself.

Two days later, Ariel sat in the rock garden with her head bowed low. Things had gotten worse. Her tears flowed freely, mixing with the salty seawater. She wished her tears could wash away her memories of that morning.

In her mind she could still see Sebastian's face as he tried to get the mermaids to do their lessons. The royal court composer had been horrified by the way they were acting. It was bad enough that Adella wouldn't speak to Alana or Aquata and that Alana gave

Aquata dirty looks, but when they'd arrived at class that morning, Arista had flatly refused to sit next to Alana!

The morning lesson was on sea life, usually one of their favorite subjects. Sebastian had asked Andrina a question. "What is the largest fish in the sea?"

"The whale," Andrina replied.

"Does anyone disagree with her answer?" Sebastian then asked the mermaids.

Attina raised her hand, and Sebastian called on her. "The largest fish can't be the whale," she said. "Whales live in the sea, but they are not fish. They're mammals."

"Show-off," Andrina muttered.

Attina turned to her in surprise. "Why did you say that, Andrina?"

Andrina made a face. "You always correct my answers. I know you think you're smarter than I am."

Attina was puzzled. "That's not true. I'm not smarter than you, and I never said that I was."

"Oh, yes you did," Andrina snapped. "And I heard all about it."

"That's impossible." Attina's voice rose. "Why, that's crazy!"

Andrina's voice got louder, too. "Okay, so now you think I'm stupid *and* crazy!"

Arista turned to Alana. "And I know what *you've* been saying about me."

"Please, Princesses!" Sebastian cried out. "Stop this at once! Pay attention!"

But Sebastian's plea was in vain. Ariel watched in despair as each of her sisters accused the others of spreading lies. She couldn't wait for the lesson to be over. She needed to be alone, to think, to try to figure out why these terrible fights were happening among her sisters.

And now, sitting on her favorite rock, she finally was alone. But not for long.

"Hello, Ariel!" a voice called.

Ariel looked up. "Hello, Arsulu."

"You look sad," Arsulu told her. Her angelfish swam around her. "I hope you're not upset about what Aquata said."

"What are you talking about?" Ariel asked.

"Oh dear," Arsulu murmured. "I thought you'd heard. I thought that's why you looked so sad. . . . Never mind." She started to move away.

"Wait!" Ariel called. "What did Aquata say?"

"It's not important," Arsulu assured her. "And I can't believe anyone would believe her, anyway. Personally, I don't think you're a spoiled brat at all." She gasped and clapped a hand over her mouth. "I'm sorry! Oh, please don't let Aquata know I told you! I'm sure she didn't mean it."

Ariel stared at her coolly. "No, I'm sure she didn't mean it," she said. Ariel knew Aquata would never say anything like that.

Arsulu smiled brightly. "Well, I must be on my way. I promised to meet Adella at the mall," she said. "Cheer up, Ariel!" She swam away with her fish following close behind. Seconds later, Flounder swam by.

"Flounder!" Ariel cried. "My dearest, most favorite friend in the whole wide sea!"

"Uh-oh," Flounder said nervously. "When you talk like that, I know you want me to do something for you."

"It's just a small teensy-weensy favor," Ariel assured him. "And it would be an adventure!"

"I'm not looking for any adventures, Ariel," Flounder protested.

"But Flounder," Ariel said sweetly. "This

will be fun. You get to be a spy. Wouldn't you like that?"

"No, I wouldn't," he replied. "I don't know anything about spying."

"It's easy!" Ariel said. "I'd do it myself, but I'd be recognized." Flounder was still shaking his head, but Ariel went on. She knew he'd eventually give in. "Did you see that mermaid who was just talking to me?"

Flounder nodded.

"Her name is Arsulu. I want you to follow her and tell me everything she does."

"Why?" Flounder asked.

"There's something strange going on," Ariel told him. "My sisters are all fighting with each other, and nobody is talking to anyone else. They started acting this way just after Arsulu came, and I think she may have something to do with it."

Now Flounder was interested. "What do you think she's done?" he asked. "Do you think she's dangerous?" He quivered slightly.

Ariel sighed. "Flounder, she's just a mermaid. She can't hurt you. Won't you help me? Please? I'm so worried about my sisters."

Flounder finally gave in. He agreed to

watch Arsulu and report back to Ariel later that afternoon.

Meanwhile, Ariel decided she was going to try to patch things up between her sisters. She went first to see Attina, who was reading in her room. Attina was still upset about what Andrina had said to her.

"Ariel, I don't think I'm smarter than anyone else. I've never said anything like that. Why would Andrina think I said that?"

"I don't know," Ariel said. "But I have a feeling it has something to do with Arsulu. Haven't you noticed how all the fighting started just after she came here?"

"That's just a coincidence," Attina said. "I think Arsulu is sweet! She gave me this great book to read the other day. She's one of the nicest people I've ever met." She frowned. "She's definitely nicer than certain sisters I know!"

Ariel could see that it was useless to talk to Attina about Arsulu. Attina's mind was set. Ariel swam over to Adella's room next. "Adella, do you think there's something particularly strange about Arsulu?"

"Don't be silly," Adella said. "She's

wonderful. I wish *she* were my sister instead of some other people."

When Ariel told Aquata her suspicions about Arsulu, Aquata became angry. "Ariel, you've had something against Arsulu ever since she arrived. Personally, I think you don't like her because she's getting so much attention from everyone."

Ariel was losing her patience. "Well, she said that you said that I was a spoiled brat! Did you say that about me?"

Aquata rolled her eyes. "Of course not. I never said that. And she never said I did. You're making that up, Ariel. You're just trying to turn me against Arsulu." She gritted her teeth. "And you can forget that. She's just about the only friend I have right now."

With Alana, Arista, and Andrina, it was the same story. From each of them, Ariel heard only praise for Arsulu. And they all scolded Ariel for criticizing Arsulu.

Ariel wondered if she should talk to her father about the situation. He'd been so busy lately that he hadn't been around much. For the past two days he hadn't even eaten dinner with them. If he had, he would have known what was going on—at dinnertime, nobody even spoke.

Ariel soon found out that King Triton already knew what was going on. Later that day, as she was sitting on her bed, gazing out the window, the King came to see her.

"Ariel," he said, "I want to speak with you."

"Yes, Father?"

"Do you know what is going on between your sisters?" he asked. "Sebastian tells me that no one is getting along. He says that everyone argued and fought all morning . . . except you. Is this true?"

"Yes, Father," Ariel replied. "But I don't know why everyone seems to be fighting."

King Triton frowned. "This is not good. It is all my fault. I should be spending more time with my daughters."

"But you have so much to do," Ariel said. "The kingdom needs your attention."

"It seems that my daughters may need my attention more," the King replied.

"Father, don't worry about us," Ariel said. "We'll work everything out." Her father already had so much on his mind that she didn't want to burden him further.

Later, she met with Flounder. "Did you follow Arsulu?" she asked eagerly. "Did you find out anything?"

"I don't understand why you don't like Arsulu," Flounder said. "She isn't mean at all!"

Ariel's heart sank at his words. "She didn't do anything evil or nasty?"

"No," Flounder replied. "There's nothing nasty about Arsulu. You want to know who's nasty? Your sister Arista!"

"Arista!" Ariel exclaimed.

"Yes. She said terrible things about you."

Ariel was stunned. "You heard Arista say terrible things about me?"

"Yes," Flounder said. "Well, no, not exactly. At the mall I heard Arsulu tell Adella that Arista said—"

"Stop!" Ariel screeched. "Flounder, don't you see what's going on? Arsulu is making up those things to pit us against each other."

"But why would she do that?" Flounder asked.

Ariel shook her head sadly. "I don't have the slightest idea." She was silent for a moment. "Come on, Flounder. You can keep me company while I make the finishing touches on my sculpture. Adella's birthday banquet is tonight, and her present has to be ready. Maybe the banquet will make her so happy that she'll forget about all the fighting and everyone will make up."

Flounder followed Ariel to the hiding place where she kept the sculpture. But when she entered the cave, she stopped short. "Oh no!" she gasped.

Ariel's beautiful coral sculpture, the gift for Adella that she'd been working on for so long, lay in pieces all over the ground. It was totally destroyed.

She heard a sound behind her and whirled around. There stood Arsulu.

Arsulu was shaking her head sadly as she looked at the chunks of coral. "Isn't that terrible."

"Yes," Ariel said, trying to keep from crying. "Terrible."

"And to think that your own sister would do such a thing," Arsulu said. "I was passing, and I saw her do it. It was so mean of her."

Ariel didn't say anything.

"Don't you want to know which of your sisters did it?" Arsulu asked.

Ariel looked at her coldly. "No."

"*I* want to know!" Flounder said.

"No, you don't," Ariel said grimly.

Arsulu shrugged. "Well, I feel so sorry for you, Ariel," she said. "I know how hard you've worked on that sculpture." She started to leave the cave. "I must be off," she said, "to search for my merman."

Ariel watched as Arsulu swam away. Then she turned back to look at her broken sculpture. Suddenly she heard a tiny voice.

"She's lying."

Ariel looked down. A snail was huddled in the sand.

"I was here," the snail said. "I saw everything."

Ariel knelt down. "Who ruined my sculpture?" she asked the snail.

But she knew the answer even before the snail told her.

Ariel may not have been surprised by the snail's answer, but Flounder certainly was. "*Arsulu* smashed your sculpture?" he asked in amazement. "It must have been an accident!"

"I don't think so, Flounder," Ariel said. She started to swim away from the cave.

"Do you want me to follow her again?" Flounder asked, swimming alongside her.

"No, thank you," Ariel replied. "Today, *I'm* going to be the spy. I have a sneaking suspicion that there is no 'beloved merman' and there never was. I want to know where Arsulu goes when she says she's searching for him."

Ariel shot through the water so fast that her tail left a stream of bubbles behind her. After a few minutes she spotted Arsulu's figure in the distance and the angelfish by her side.

Ariel stayed as far back as she could while still keeping an eye on Arsulu. She told herself she had nothing to fear and that Arsulu was just another mermaid. But her heart was pounding rapidly just the same.

Arsulu began to swim faster, and Ariel had to swim furiously to keep up. She swam on and on, beyond the palace, beyond all the familiar sights. After a while she found herself deep in a part of the sea that she'd never explored.

There was a reason for that. These waters were dark and gloomy, thick with brown tangled weeds and vines. There was no sign of any other sea creatures anywhere. The silence was eerie. Although she kept a safe distance behind Arsulu, Ariel hoped the swish of her tail wouldn't give her away.

For a second she thought Arsulu had disappeared. Then she saw the last bit of the mermaid's tail dart into a cave.

Ariel slowed her pace and moved toward the side of the cave. Carefully she crept around to the entrance. Hiding behind a shrub, she peered inside.

Arsulu was pacing in the cave, talking to her fish. "My dear Flotsam, my darling Jetsam! My scheme is working exactly as planned. Slowly but surely, I have managed to pit each dreadful sister against the other. Soon they will all despise each other, and my plan will be a complete success!"

Ariel listened in utter confusion. She wasn't surprised to hear that Arsulu was responsible for the fighting among the mermaids. That was just what she suspected. The question was—*why*? Why was she doing this to the family? What did she have to gain?

"I know that Triton must see how his daughters are misbehaving," Arsulu continued. "He has to be worried about them. How can he think about his kingdom when there is such a grand conflict going on in his own home? It is nearly the perfect time to make my move. Before he even knows what has happened, the kingdom will be mine!"

She's mad, Ariel thought. How could one young mermaid possibly take over the kingdom?

Arsulu threw back her head and laughed loudly. But it wasn't the pretty, tinkling laugh Ariel had heard from her before. This laugh was more like a deep, throaty cackle. "Yes, my pretty eels," she bellowed. "Triton will rue the day he crossed my path. My revenge is close at hand!"

Ariel blinked. Eels? What was she talking about? She watched as Arsulu lifted a mirror. "Soon, very soon, the merpeople of the sea will bow to *me*. Triton and his wretched daughters will be my slaves!"

An angelfish crossed in front of the mirror. Ariel gasped. In the mirror, what she saw was not the reflection of a sweet angelfish but that of an evil eel! Then Arsulu brought the mirror to her own face. And there, in the mirror's reflection, was not the face of a beautiful fair-haired mermaid; instead, it was a horrid, grotesque, ugly face—a face of pure evil. Ariel had to put a hand to her mouth to keep from screaming.

The ghoulish face in the mirror grinned.

"All will hail Ursula the Sea Witch, ruler of the seas!"

Ariel backed away from the cave, shaking with fright. Then she swam as fast as she could back toward the palace.

When she was a safe distance away, she ducked into a cave to catch her breath and collect her thoughts.

This was unbelievable, unbelievable! But she'd seen it with her own eyes. Arsulu—whom the princesses thought was a charming, lovely mermaid—was really Ursula the Sea Witch, their father's most feared enemy! And all the problems they were having were Ursula's fault, part of her plot to take over King Triton's kingdom!

I can't believe how dumb I've been, Ariel thought. Why, even the letters in Arsulu's name spell it out—rearranged, *Arsulu* is *Ursula!*

Ariel was still shaking, but she knew she couldn't rest for much longer. Who knew what Arsulu/Ursula would be up to next? She had to get back and warn everyone. She hoped that it wasn't too late.

8

Racing through the waters and into the palace, Ariel searched for any sign of her father or her sisters. When she spotted Arista and Attina, she hurried toward them.

"Where's Father?" she asked breathlessly.

Neither responded to her question. They were too busy yelling at each other to pay attention.

"Arsulu gave *me* the book," Attina shouted.

"She did not!" Arista screeched. "She gave it to me first! If you want it, you'll have to wait until I'm through with it."

Ariel pushed herself between them. "Wait! Listen to me! Do you know why you're fighting? It's all because of Arsulu. She's been spreading lies and changing the names on the chart and doing all kinds of tricks to turn us against each other!"

Arista and Attina were stunned. They stared at Ariel in disbelief.

"And you want to know why she's doing that to us?" Ariel went on. "Because she's not really Arsulu—she's Ursula the Sea Witch!"

There was a moment of silence. Then Arista rolled her eyes. "Ariel, that's ridiculous. Don't talk nonsense."

"You shouldn't make up stories like that," Attina scolded. "I always knew you had a vivid imagination, but now you're carrying it too far!"

"I'm not making it up," Ariel protested. "It's true. I saw her! We have to warn Father!" She saw Aquata and waved for her to join them.

"What do you want?" Aquata asked impatiently.

Ariel repeated what she'd just told Attina

and Arista. "Aquata, remember when we were in your room, and Alana was showing you the jewelry box with the mirror that she got for Adella? Remember how Arsulu left the room so suddenly? Now I know why! She can't look in a mirror because the reflection would show who she really is! She's really Ursula the Sea Witch!"

Aquata wasn't the least bit impressed with Ariel's news. "Sure, Ariel," she said in a scornful voice. "Arsulu is a sea witch."

"She is!" Ariel cried. "And not just any sea witch. She's Ursula! I'm telling you the truth. You have to listen to me. This is all part of her plot. Arsulu, I mean Ursula, wants to take over the kingdom!"

Aquata burst out laughing. The sound of her laughter drew Adella, Andrina, and Alana. Adella glared at Aquata. "What's so funny? Are you making fun of me again?"

Aquata sneered at her. "No, I'm making fun of Ariel. Wait till you hear this wild story she's telling. She says Arsulu is really Ursula the Sea Witch, and she's trying to take over the kingdom."

Andrina groaned. "Ariel, you've been

down on Arsulu ever since she came. What have you got against her, anyway? What did she ever do to you?"

Alana sniffed. "You just hate that we all like her so much. You're jealous."

"Yeah," Arista said. "You're used to getting all the attention."

"We are not going to listen to your nasty story," Attina declared.

"It's the truth," Ariel said yet again. "I have to tell Father. She's evil!"

Adella was outraged. "How dare you speak like that about my best friend."

"*Your* best friend?" Aquata gritted her teeth. "She's *my* best friend."

That remark made Adella even more furious. "I guess it's not enough that you stole my merman. Now you're trying to steal my best friend. Remember, *I* met her first! She's *my* best friend."

"What about me?" Alana broke in. "She's *my* best friend."

"I doubt that," Arista said. "Just because she went shopping with you once doesn't mean you're best friends. And anyway, I'm closer to her than you are. I was even planning to ask Father if I could invite her to Adella's birthday banquet tonight."

"But I was going to ask Father that!" Adella declared. Suddenly they were all fighting over whose best friend Arsulu was and who would invite her to the banquet.

Ariel was beginning to panic. "Please! Don't you see what's happening? We never fought like this before she came here!"

But no one was listening to her. Ariel clutched her head in despair. It was hopeless. "I'm going to find Father," she declared, and took off.

No one even noticed that she had gone. They were too busy fighting and yelling at each other.

"She likes me better than you!" Adella shrieked at Aquata.

"No, she likes me best!" Aquata yelled back.

"Please don't fight!" called a sweet, pleading voice. "I love you all!" The sisters turned to see Arsulu rushing toward them.

Suddenly the voice of King Triton boomed out. "Stop this quarreling at once!" As he strode toward them, the anger on his face was clear. "What is the meaning of this constant yelling and screaming?"

"It's all Ariel's fault," Arista cried out. "She's saying nasty things about Arsulu." She looked around. "Where did Ariel go?"

"Arsulu?" King Triton asked. "Who is Arsulu?"

Adella put her arm around the impostor. "*This* is Arsulu. We told you, Father. She's traveling through our kingdom, and we've invited her to stay."

"Ah yes, I remember," King Triton said. "How do you do, Arsulu."

Arsulu bowed low. "I am honored to meet the great and noble King Triton, ruler of the seas."

"It is a pleasure to have you here, Arsulu," King Triton said. "I saw how you tried to make peace among my daughters, and I am very grateful." Then, to the mermaids, he said, "I demand to know what is going on!"

"She started it," Adella wailed, pointing at Aquata.

"Andrina's been spreading lies about me," Alana cried out.

"Enough!" Triton roared. "Today is

Adella's birthday," he said in a calmer voice. "At the banquet tonight you will behave as loving sisters. There will be no fighting and no name-calling—only kind words. Is that understood?"

"Yes, Father," they all answered meekly.

Adella stepped forward. "Father, can Arsulu come to the banquet? Since it's my birthday and she's my best friend—"

"*Your* best friend," Aquata sputtered, but a look from her father silenced her.

"She's like a sister to us," Adella continued.

"Of course she can come," King Triton said.

Once again Arsulu bowed. "I am grateful, O gracious and glorious king."

Fixing one more stern look at his daughters, King Triton left the palace.

Ariel lay on her bed, scared and tense. She'd searched the grounds at the palace—both inside and out—but she hadn't been able to find her father. Now she was truly frightened. Her sisters hadn't believed her. What if her own father didn't believe her, either?

When she felt a ripple, she turned eagerly

to see if perhaps one of her sisters or her father was coming in. But when she saw who was floating in her doorway, her stomach did flip-flops. It was Arsulu.

The phony mermaid sidled over to her. "What unkind things have you been saying about me, Ariel?" she asked. Her lips curled upward. It was the same evil grin Ariel had seen in the cave.

Ariel hoped her hands weren't shaking too much. "I know who you are, *Ursula*."

Arsulu didn't bat an eye. "But no one else does, my dear," she said, giving Ariel an evil stare. "And no one will believe you. When I am ruler of the seas, I have special plans just for you, Ariel."

Ariel's whole body was trembling. What if Ursula tried to hurt her right then? Ariel didn't have the power to fight the Sea Witch. Only her father had that power . . . and he was nowhere to be found! She quickly jumped off her bed and fled from the palace. Arsulu did not follow her.

What am I going to do? she asked herself as she swam away. I have to prove to them that she is really Ursula. But how?

Ariel settled down on a large rock to think. I could bring a mirror to the banquet tonight, she thought. Then they'd all see the truth for themselves. But she knew that wouldn't work. Ursula was too smart to be tricked into looking at a mirror.

Ariel was so frightened and depressed that she began to cry. The kingdom would be lost. Her father, her sisters, and she would all become slaves . . . or worse.

She sat there for a long time until she realized it was getting late. It was almost time for the banquet, and she had to get back to the palace. Surely by now her father would be there and she could tell him about Ursula. But would she be able to convince him? What if her sisters insisted she was lying?

A school of goldfish were coming toward her as she got up from the rock. "Good evening, Princess Ariel," they said in unison.

"Good evening," Ariel murmured, barely seeing them. As they passed, she was dimly aware of how shiny they were. She could see her reflection in their scales.

Suddenly an idea exploded in her mind.
"Goldfish!" she cried out. "Wait!"

9

The banquet hall at the royal palace was beautifully decorated for Adella's birthday. Colorful streamers and shiny pearls hung from the walls. In the center a head table was set up, with a smaller table on each side. All three tables were set with the finest silver and china, and each was covered with magnificent lilies.

Ariel's sisters and Arsulu filed into the huge room, "Oohing" and "Aahing" at the marvelous arrangement. All was fine until a small argument broke out among the sisters as they all fought to sit next to Arsulu. The arrival of King Triton quickly put an end to that.

"Greetings, my daughters," he said. "A happy birthday to you, Adella. And welcome to our guest, Arsulu." He smiled at them all, but his forehead was lined with worry. "Before the festivities begin, I have something very important to say."

He paused, and the mermaids gave him their full attention. When he spoke, his voice was serious. "I am worried about you all. It is not right for sisters as close as you to fight as you have been doing. I know that I am partly to blame," he added. "Perhaps if I had spent more time with you, none of this would have happened. That is why I have decided to take you away with me on a grand holiday to another sea."

"A vacation!" the mermaids squealed with delight.

"Ooh, Father," Arista cried. "Can we go to the Mediterranean? It's so glamorous!"

"No, let's go to the Caribbean!" Alana argued.

"No, the Arctic!" Andrina called out.

"But Father," Aquata broke in. "Who will watch over the kingdom?"

King Triton smiled at his eldest daughter. "Surely the kingdom can survive without me for a short time," he said.

Arsulu nodded with approval. "I think you are a wonderful father, King Triton."

"Thank you, Arsulu," King Triton said. "Now, let us celebrate Adella's birthday." Suddenly he noticed somebody was missing. "Where is Ariel?" he asked.

"Late," Alana said.

"As usual," Aquata added.

"She wants to ruin everything," Adella muttered. "Even my birthday."

"Can't we start dinner without her, Father?" Andrina asked.

"I suppose so," King Triton said. "That daughter of mine must be taught a lesson! Her constant tardiness is inexcusable."

And so the banquet began. Delicious food was served, and while everyone ate, there was peace for a change. The mermaids couldn't argue with their mouths full.

When the birthday cake came out, Ariel

was still not there. Everyone sang happy birthday to a beaming Adella, and she blew out her candles.

But King Triton was growing worried. "Where *is* Ariel?" he asked again. "It's not like her to miss a birthday banquet."

"Father," Adella said, "could Arsulu come with us on our holiday?"

Before King Triton could reply, Arsulu said, "That's very kind of you, Adella. But I would prefer to stay here. I still haven't given up trying to find my merman."

Aquata turned to King Triton. "Arsulu was engaged to marry," she explained. "But the Sea Witch chased him from their sea. Arsulu has been searching for him ever since."

King Triton's eyes grew dark. "Ursula," he grumbled. "She is an evil and horrid creature. No one is safe in her presence."

"Yes," Arsulu said. "I know."

As they ate birthday cake, there was only one tiny quarrel, started when Andrina saw that Arista had a bigger piece than she did. King Triton cast a stern glance at his daughters, and they stopped arguing at once. "It is time to give Adella her gifts," he announced. One by one the mermaids swam over to Adella and presented her with a birthday present.

"*Two* jewelry boxes!" Adella exclaimed when she opened the gifts from Arista and Alana. Opening the lid of one of them, she examined herself in its built-in mirror.

"I bought mine first," Alana growled, glaring at Arista.

"You did not," Arista shot back.

"Oh well," Adella said, "I suppose I can give one to Arsulu, since she's my dearest friend. Here, Arsulu." She extended the open jewelry box across the table toward her.

"Oh, no thank you, dear Adella," Arsulu said, quickly shutting the lid and handing it back. "I couldn't bear to take away your sister's gift."

At that moment Ariel burst into the banquet hall.

"Well, it's about time!" King Triton declared. "Ariel, you are very late!"

"But Father," Ariel said. "I must tell you—"

"Silence!" King Triton roared. "I don't want to hear any excuses from you. We are giving Adella her birthday gifts. I hope, at

71

least, that you have one for her."

Ariel took a deep breath. "Adella," she said. "I was making a beautiful coral sculpture for your birthday. Unfortunately, something happened to it."

"Hah," Adella muttered. "You probably just forgot to get me anything, and you're making up excuses."

Ariel heard her sister's comments but ignored them. "So I have a different gift for you," she continued. "It is a special performance created in honor of your birthday." She rose and held out her arm. "Behold! The amazing dancing goldfish!"

A stream of large, glittering goldfish came fluttering into the room, followed by Octavio, Sebastian's chief musician. Octavio was the only octopus in the kingdom who could play four fiddles at once. He lifted the instruments and struck up a song, and the fish began to dance in a circle.

Slowly a smile crept up on Adella's face. She thought the fish were beautiful. Everyone, even the King, rose from the table and gathered around to watch.

The goldfish formed a line and circled

Adella. She giggled happily as they danced a ring around her. Everyone clapped along with the music as the fish honored the birthday mermaid. Then they circled Arista and danced around her, too. To everyone's delight, the fish danced around each of the sisters, one after the other.

Ariel kept her eyes on Arsulu/Ursula the entire time. At first the phony mermaid clapped along with everyone else. Then the goldfish started toward her. She backed away, but the fish moved quickly and formed a circle around her, anyway.

Ariel had been waiting for this moment. "Look!" she cried, pointing to the goldfish. "Look at their scales!"

The reflection in their scales was a little blurry, but there was no question as to whose reflection it was. Even distorted, there was no mistaking the grotesque image of Ursula the Sea Witch. A scream of horror went up from the sisters.

King Triton's face became red, then purple with fury. "Ursula!" he roared.

Images of the ugly Sea Witch flashed by in every goldfish that danced around her.

Ursula tried to get away, but the fish moved closer together, tightening the circle.

They moved faster and faster around her—so fast that they formed a current that forced Ursula to spin. A loud, shrill scream echoed throughout the banquet hall as the goldfish began to move their spinning circle, lifting Ursula up and out of the palace. Her screeching became fainter and fainter as the goldfish carried her far from the kingdom.

The banquet hall was silent. The mermaids were all in a state of shock as they tried to absorb what had just happened before their very eyes.

"Oh, Ariel," Adella wailed. "You were right!"

"How could we have been so foolish?" Alana asked.

"I should have seen right through her," Aquata said mournfully.

Arista turned to Andrina. "I'm sorry I called you names."

"And I'm sorry I met your merman," Aquata told Adella.

Ariel stayed off to one side and watched as Aquata made up with Adella and as Arista gave Andrina an enormous hug. All at once, everyone began apologizing to one another, crying and hugging—everyone but Ariel. She put her hands on her hips. "Hey!" she shouted to her sisters.

Everyone became quiet, and all eyes turned to Ariel. "What about *me*?" she asked, holding her arms out and waiting for them to come rushing over with hugs for her, too.

The princesses looked at each other and giggled softly. "What *about* you?" Alana asked, trying to hide her smile.

Ariel was shocked! Why, *she* was the one responsible for their making up in the first place! How rude of them to not even give her one single hug or apologize for being so nasty. Insulted, she spun around and headed for the door.

"Ariel!" they called. "Wait!"

Ariel turned back to see all six of her sisters swimming toward her with huge smiles on their faces.

"Ariel!" Aquata exclaimed, "We could *never* forget you!"

The next thing she knew, Ariel was being showered with kisses and hugs and a chorus of "I'm sorry's." It got so noisy with all the laughter and chattering that the mermaids didn't even hear their father approach. When they finally did notice him, they moved away from Ariel so that he could speak to her.

"Ariel, my dear," he said warmly. "You have saved the kingdom and reunited our family. For that, we all thank you from the bottom of our hearts." He gave Ariel a big hug and a kiss on her forehead. "And as a special thank you for your heroic deed," he declared, "we shall throw a grand banquet in your honor!"

The mermaids clapped their hands together and beamed with happiness. But it was Ariel who wore the biggest smile of all. She couldn't help but feel proud of herself. She had single-handedly saved the kingdom and her family—not a bad day's work for a little mermaid.